This Book Was Given With Love To:

Copyright © 2020 by Puppy Dogs & Ice Cream, Inc.
All rights reserved. Published in the United States
by Puppy Dogs & Ice Cream, Inc.
ISBN: 978-1-953177-50-6
Edition: October 2020

For all inquiries, please contact us at:
info@puppysmiles.org

To see more of our books, visit us at:
www.PuppyDogsAndIceCream.com

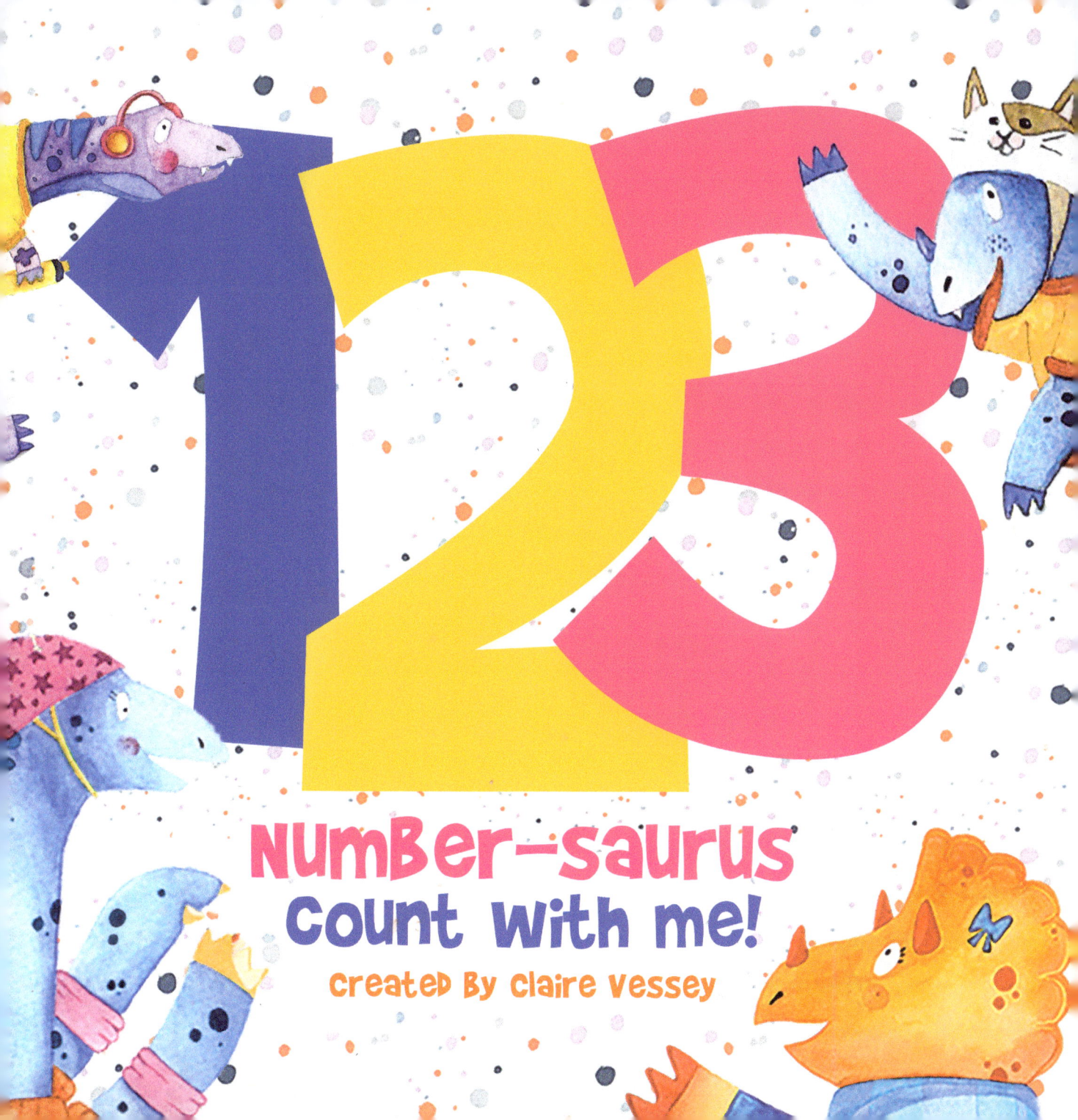

1

One lucky dinosaur
out on his scooter.
You can hear him coming
when he TOOTS his hooter.

Here come dinosaurs
2 and 3.
Riding on their tandem bike
down the hill with a "WHEEEEEE!!!"

4

This is dinosaur
number four.
Zooming on a skateboard is a
GREAT BIG Brontosaur.

5

Number five loves rollerskating,
even in the rain.
She SPLISHES and she SPLOSHES,
then she does it all again.

6 & 7

Grandpa and baby
are in their own heaven.
Cycling through the park,
they are numbers six and seven.

8

Running to the picnic
is dino number eight.
POUNDING down the footpath,
he simply can't be late!

9

Here is handstanding
number nine.
She WIBBLES and she WOBBLES,
but she'll never fall... She's fine.

10

Arriving in sporty style
ten is the last to the picnic.
Waving as she comes in for a landing,
and looking quite fantastic.

The sun is shining,
and everyone is here.
Now let's all give
a really big cheer...

One, two, three, four, five
six, seven, eight, nine, ten...

HOORAY!!!

Can you count all ten dinos?

 **Claim Your FREE Gift!**

Visit ➡ PDICBooks.com/Gift

Thank you for purchasing "123 Number-Saurus Count with Me," and welcome to the Puppy Dogs & Ice Cream family.

We're certain you're going to love the little gift we've prepared for you at the website above.

CPSIA information can be obtained
at www.ICGtesting.com
Printed in the USA
LVHW070851151120
671749LV00011B/139